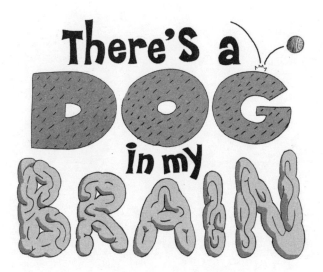

There's a DOG in my BRAIN

Caroline Green

illustrated by Rikin Parekh

WALKER
BOOKS

First published 2022 by Walker Books Ltd
87 Vauxhall Walk, London SE11 5HJ

2 4 6 8 10 9 7 5 3 1

Text © 2022 Caroline Green
Illustrations © 2022 Rikin Parekh

The right of Caroline Green and Rikin Parekh
to be identified as author and illustrator respectively
of this work has been asserted in accordance
with the Copyright, Designs and Patents Act 1988

This book has been typeset in Nimrod, Johann and Zalderdash

Printed and bound by CPI Group (UK) Ltd, Croydon CR0 4YY

British Library Cataloguing in Publication Data:
a catalogue record for this book is available
from the British Library

ISBN 978-1-4063-9943-1

www.walker.co.uk

MIX
Paper from
responsible sources
FSC® C171272
www.fsc.org

For Monty. A lovely boy and a lovely friend.

C. G.

For Bella and Nanu X

R. P.

Danny Pond is quite comfortable down by the dog basket, thank you very much.

It's fair to say that it's a bit whiffy. OK, it's *extremely* whiffy. On a scale of one to ten, with your mum's lovely chocolate sponge cake in top spot at number one, and something terrible on your shoe at number ten, this mix of doggy smells, fish breath and hint of blow-off is a solid eight.

But Danny doesn't care. What's a bit of a pong between best mates?

Dudley the dog gives one of his contented sighs. His droopy chops puff out then shiver back into place. Dad says Dudley is "Part Labrador, part poodle, part rug. But mostly idiot."

(Rude.) As far as Danny is concerned, Dudley

is the **CUDDLIEST, FUNNIEST, BESTEST** dog in the world.

Dudley is the last thing Danny sees at night, curled on his bed, trumpeting snores like an engine – and every morning begins with Dudley's big, pink tongue sandpapering Danny's sleepy face, dog breath blasting up his nostrils.

The two of them are so close that Mum says she doesn't know where the boy ends and the dog begins.

"Come on, boy." Danny gives Dudley a gentle nudge. "Can't put this off any longer."

They both clamber up and head for the back door. One last visit to the garden and then Danny has to leave Dudley to his fate. He doesn't want to go.

It's so unfair. If Danny has to go to this stupid family wedding, why can't Dudley come too? Why aren't dogs at weddings A Thing?

Better yet, they could both stay home.

Imagine! A weekend with just the two of them. He could sleep in Dudley's basket, feed Dudley bits of dinner off his plate without anyone telling him off and they could play chase in the park. Instead, Mrs Grout from down the road is coming to stay because she has the decorators in – his mum couldn't have picked anyone **WORSE!**

For a start, Mrs Grout has always looked at Dudley like he's the very worst dog in the world rather than the best. She always says, "I'm more of a cat person..." as she tries to squinch as far away as she can from friendly old Dudley like he's a T-Rex about to eat her.

When it was all arranged the other day,

Danny overheard her murmuring, "I'm going to sort you out once and for all, you hairy mutt."

Even going to a boring wedding and hanging out with his football-obsessed cousin, Priya, is better than a weekend with Mrs Grout.

"Sorry, boy," Danny says, as he watches Dudley do his business, his doggy face as serious as if he is doing really hard maths in his head. After he's done, Dudley ambles over to where Danny is sitting on the back step and lies down at his feet. Danny stares into Dudley's sad brown eyes. They always look like that, even if he's just done one of his favourite things like rolling in fox poo, or stealing ice cream from a toddler's hand.

"Wish *I* could stay instead of you, old friend," whispers Danny, ruffling the special spot behind Dudley's ear. The dog's tail thump-thump-thumps and he instantly starts snoring, like someone flipped a switch from **AWAKE** to **ASLEEP** in his brain.

Gazing up at the velvety darkness above, Danny looks for the Pup Star, the one Dad told him is the brightest star in the sky. His dad is full of facts about the sky. He once told Danny that really, really (really) bright stars sometimes get *too* bright. When that happens, they chuck off some of their stardust into the atmosphere. A bit like when Dudley sheds clumps of his hair and it rolls around like tumbleweed in the hall.

So what if, right now, the Pup Star is doing the exploding thing? Just as Danny makes a wish? Maybe a little stardust can make his wish come true? It might sound daft, but Danny is getting desperate. Got to be worth a try.

He lifts his face to the sky.

I wish ...

... I wish I could find a way to stay behind instead of Dudley!

Nothing happens ...

... still nothing ...

... but wait!

... Nope.

Danny scrunches his face up, wishing so hard this time that it gives him a pain in both ears, a bit of a headache and he almost does a tiny wee.

Let me stay behind instead of Dudley! PLEASE!

And then...

Something shivery passes through Danny's head. He feels it fizz and whirl inside him ...

... down and down and down ...

... through his insides ...

... past his heart, lungs, spleen and all the other gross squishy stuff in there ...

... and right down to his shoes.

It sounds like millions of dogs are barking all at once, inside *and* outside Danny's head. Then he's falling, falling...

2

The *smell* is the first thing.

Except that word doesn't really do it justice. It's not one smell – this is a symphony of smells, a pandemonium of pongs, a whirlwind of whiffs, all bombarding Danny's nose at once.

He opens his eyes.

That's when he realises he is still curled up in Dudley's bed. Is that the reason the world has turned so smelly?

That's weird...

He should be sitting in the back of the car on his way to a hotel for the night.

Danny lifts his arm to check his watch, the cool one with the chunky face that Grandma gave him last Christmas ...

... and finds himself looking down at a great big, hairy, grey paw instead.

Nope. That's not right.

He closes his eyes, hoping this will reset his brain.

I'm dreaming. Definitely dreaming. When I open my eyes, I'll see my own arm. I'll see my watch and the sleeve of my red hoodie with that little hole I stick my thumb through when I feel nervous.

Danny opens his eyes. He's still looking at a great big, hairy, grey paw.

Lifting it up in astonishment, the paw finds the back of his left ear like it's magnetised. The next thing he knows, Danny is having the most

16

satisfying scratch he has ever had in his life.
Who knew scratching felt so *good*?

MUST CONCENTRATE.

Before he gets any more confused, Danny
dashes upstairs at top speed to Mum and Dad's
room to look in their big mirror. Jumping on the
bed, he sees their pure white duvet has muddy
marks on it that weren't there a second ago.

Strange. You'd almost think *he*
made them.

"**COME BACK
HERE AT
ONCE!**" shouts a
voice so harsh that
it's like having a
scratchy dish cloth
rubbed inside his
ear. "You're not
allowed upstairs,
you filthy beast!"

Eh? That's a bit strong.

But something is very, *very* wrong…

Because looking back at him in the mirror isn't a boy with scruffy brown hair, a mole on his cheek and blue eyes.

It is a large, grey, hairy dog with a very shocked expression.

"**HELP!**" says Danny miserably.

Unfortunately, all that comes out is a single, sad, "Woof."

3

Something has happened to Dudley's sniff. Has it got broke? He knows he's in the horrible vroom-vroom thing by the roaring sound and the way he feels sick. But it doesn't smell right.

Dudley doesn't know why he's here. He was snoozing on Danny's knee. (Which he liked.) Now he's here. (Which he doesn't like.)

He tries his sniff again, pressing his nose to the seat in front, but everything smells *wrong*,

like someone has washed all the lovely pongs
away. Then he spots something on the fabric.
Food? He pokes out his tongue and gives it a
good lick.

Hmmm … tastes a bit strange. Has his lick
got broke too?

"*Danny?*"

Dudley gets such a shock he almost tumbles off the seat.

"**WHAT ON EARTH** are you doing licking the back of your dad's seat?!" Dudley knows that voice. It's the Mum. "And put your seatbelt on!"

Dudley cringes in his seat. He hates shouty, cross voices. He tries to flatten his hearing flappers so the noise is less hurty, but they won't work properly either. None of his bits seem to work any more.

"I'm sure we should have turned off by now. Can you look at Google maps?"

Dudley knows that voice too. But the Dad isn't talking to Dudley.

Dudley looks down at himself.

Well, those aren't *Dudley's* leggies.

Where've his leggies gone?

And, hang on, where've his paws gone?

Where's his belly gone?

Where's DUDLEY GONE?

He needs Danny. Danny will sort it out! Danny will rub his ears and say, "Who's the best dog then? You are!" Which is totally true, so Dudley will wag his tail in agreement.

Hang on. Speaking of waggy tails...

WHERE'S DUDLEY'S TAIL GONE???!!!

Dudley experimentally lifts one of the all-wrong legs and gives it a shake. He tries to whine but it comes out sounding like that time he had "a-bad-case-of-kennel-cough-I'm-afraid".

"You OK back there?" The Mum turns to look at him. "Danny?"

DANNY? Where? Dudley looks around but can't see him.

"Can you check those directions again?" says the Dad. "I really think we're lost."

"Hang on," she says. The Mum reaches over and clicks the funny belt thing over Dudley then turns around. "Let me have another look..."

No one is paying any attention to Dudley now.

His chin falls forwards, but he can't smell anything at all.

There's no mistake: his sniff has definitely got broke... But nevermind, the window's open.

This is **BRILLIANT!**

Danny stares down at the bowl of dried, stinky stuff and then up at Mrs Grout.

"Do you really expect me to eat *that*?" he says. Or tries to.

"Don't you growl at me, you naughty dog," says Mrs Grout. "If you were mine, you wouldn't even be allowed in the house."

If I was yours, I'd run away and never come back.

But Danny keeps this thought inside his head because finally, one hour and three minutes (according to the clock on the cooker) after it happened, he is starting to accept that he really is inside Dudley's body.

The bad news is … well, he's a *dog* (pay attention!) but the good news is that he can now keep a proper eye on Mrs Grout and her evil plans.

And Danny has to admit that *is* quite interesting being a dog.

Earlier he spent some time exploring the inside of Dad's trainers, which smelled exactly like the cheese counter at the supermarket. Except in a good way. Who knew that he would enjoy smelling cheesy trainers so much? He was even tempted to have a tiny nibble at one point, until he had a stern word with himself.

MUST REMEMBER:
BOY NOT DOG!

Then there are his new ears. It's like they belong to a superhero whose power is hearing. (Which is a rubbish superpower.) But still. He can now hear everything from the protests of the little yappy dog who lives a whole street away, to the distant hum of a plane overhead, to a *scritch-scritch-scritch* inside the walls. (Mice?) He's discovering there's a whole other world that exists beyond the one Danny thought he knew so well.

But Danny doesn't have time to enjoy it. He needs to concentrate on watching Mrs Grout. (Who smells of horrible chemicals. All the lavender and pine and bleachy stinks mixed together are making his nose hurt. There's another smell too ... but he can't quite work that one out. It's sort of vinegary and familiar, but in a bad way that makes him feel nervous.)

Anyway, he needs to keep an eye on her. To do that, Danny must keep his strength up.

He gives the bowl an experimental sniff. Hmm ... not as bad as you'd think considering it's hard, dry chunks of Doggie-Yum-Yum that usually smells like hamster poo to Danny. Today it smells uncannily like juicy chicken glistening with lovely meaty gravy. And wait, what's that? A hint of crispy golden roast potato *too*?!

Better give it a go. Danny squeezes his eyes closed and gently picks up a chunk in his mouth.

Not bad. Not bad at all. Let's try another...

Within about ten seconds he's scoffed the lot –
less like eating and more like hoovering with his
mouth. He's thirsty now, so he has a huge drink
of water from the bowl, trying really hard to
ignore the thready bits of slimy slobber floating
in there.

After all that food and water Danny feels a bit
too full and his tum is making gurgling noises.

Oh dear.

He can't hold it in any
longer...

PAAAAAARP!

"**You disgusting
DOG!**"

shrieks Mrs
Grout,
slapping a
tea towel
over her
face.

"Eurgh! What a smell! **FILTHY, FILTHY BEAST!**"

Before Danny realises what's happening, Mrs Grout has pushed him out onto the doorstep and slammed the door behind him.

He looks up at the black clouds clumping together like one big bruise.

Pressing his nose against the glass pane of the back door, he can see Mrs Grout's bottom in front of the cooker. He gives a whine as fat drops of rain begin to plop onto his head.

He should be inside, warm and dry. Actually, he should be at a hotel...

Not for the first time, Danny wonders what is happening with Dudley.

Danny hopes, sincerely, that he is being a good boy.

Somehow he doubts it.

5

Nope. Nothing.

"Where's Danny?"

Dudley wishes he knew. He turns to look at the Mum and the Dad hopefully, but all they're doing is looking at him.

"What are you doing by that hedge?" says the Dad.

"Are you smelling the flowers?" says the Mum. "That's nice, dear."

31

Dudley gives a huffy snort and turns himself away.

This is more than any dog should have to bear.

He had been dying to get out of the vroom-vroom thing. And when they stopped, he tumbled out into a big space with green all around – great!

But now he finds there's *absolutely nowhere to do a wee*!

Not that bush, or that flowerbed. How is a dog supposed to wee when NOWHERE smells right?

He lifts a leg experimentally...

"DANNY! WHAT ARE YOU DOING?" says the Mum in a loud and high and hurty voice. "Oh my word! Can't you wait until you reach a bathroom?"

Both the Mum and the Dad have circle mouths and eyes.

Dudley narrows his eyes. He's not allowed to wee in a bathroom normally! And why is she calling Dudley *Danny* and not calling Dudley *Dudley?* Danny is Danny and Dudley is Dudley. Otherwise, where would everyone be?

It's so confusing it's giving Dudley a throbby head.

"Come on," says the Dad. "Let's get checked in. Danny, stay close."

Dudley supposes that means *him*.

Dudley trots after them into the biggest house he has ever seen. He gives a sniff. It smells of boring CLEAN like when the Dad uses the scary-bendy-tube monster and says "scooch over a bit, Dudley, and let me get under the sofa!" or "it's only a vacuum cleaner, you silly dog".

They walk down a long room with doors on each side. So many exciting places to sniff! *But no sniff to sniff them with.*

"So we're getting straight to bed now because tomorrow will be a long day." The Mum is the one doing the talking. "In the morning, after breakfast, we're going to the church for the service. Then we're coming back to the hotel for the reception. Are you even listening, Danny? *Danny?*"

She's looking at him, all frowny.

Dudley's so fed up he opens his mouth to woof,

but something else comes out instead. Something so surprising, that he tries it again.

"*DUDLEY!*" He can say his own name! What a clever, clever boy he is!

WOW!

But the Mum doesn't tell him he is a clever, clever boy.

"I've never heard such a scratchy throat! Have you got tonsillitis again?" She puts her hand on Dudley's face, which feels nice, so he pokes out his tongue and gives it a big lick.

The Mum makes a high-pitched squeak and snatches her hand away.

"Kev," she says. "He just tried to lick my hand. I think there's something seriously wrong with him."

The Dad peers into his eyes. Dudley gives a little whine.

"Hmm," he says. "Let's get you straight to bed. Maybe a good night's sleep will sort you out."

The Dad opens a door to a room with the sort of beds that Dudley's not meant to go on – and Dudley's lovely smelly dog bed isn't even there!

But it's not all bad. Dudley sees something tasty-looking on a table. Using his mouth, he picks it up and begins to munch. Bit chewy, bit crackly, bit … strange, but still delicious!

That finished, he wanders into the room with the flushing thing and goes to take a nice drink from the big white bowl.

Just as his lips reach the water, angry shouty voices are all around him.

"Daaaaaaannnnny! What on Earth do you think you're *doing*?!"

"WHAT THE HECK?"

The Mum and the Dad are staring at him in a bad way. Instead of circle eyes and mouths, their faces are all narrow angry lines, worse than "the time Dudley did a big poo on the brand-new white rug" bad. Even worse than "the time Dudley stole all the ice cream from the Year 5 picnic".

This is much, *much* worse.

"Danny," says the Dad. "Did you just eat a packet of biscuits that were still inside the wrapper?"

The Mum is breathing funny and her face looks weird. "... And then try to **DRINK FROM THE TOILET BOWL?**"

When Danny wakes up the next morning, he wonders where his duvet is – and his pillow and, well, his whole bedroom.

Then he remembers. He is a dog. He's in Dudley's basket in the hallway.

What if he gets stuck like this for ever? Will Dudley-as-Danny have to go to school, while he stays at home, sleeping all day? (Hmm, that doesn't sound too bad, actually...)

Then he pictures Dudley, dressed in Danny's school uniform, sitting in a classroom. Dudley wouldn't be able to sit still, let alone do spellings or maths! He would probably run around trying to lick people or go on a hunt for everyone's packed lunches.

Danny is distracted by a stinging, fizzy, horrible assault to his nostrils. It's coming from the kitchen. Mrs Grout is bleaching something. Cleaning seems to be her main activity. If she isn't bleaching, she's polishing. The smell is so strong it brings on a gigantic sneeze that makes all four of his legs go straight out at once. All but one back leg settles down again. It quivers in midair like it's on strings, before finding a spot behind his ear and giving it a good old scratch.

Danny wonders why he's never spent much time scratching (it is *so* wonderfully satisfying), when Mrs Grout comes into the hallway. She's wearing a tent-like dressing gown, which is pink and fluffy and topped off with a scowl.

She looks down at Danny (still scratching) like she's just smelled old socks.

"There'll be no more of *that* by the end of today, I can tell you," she hisses, before marching back into the kitchen.

Danny's insides go icy. He knew it! She really is going to get rid of Dudley! (Or Danny? Or … both of them?!) He feels all his anger twist together into a tight ball and a low growl comes out of his mouth.

Mrs Grout whirls round and waves a duster at him.

"I always knew you were a **VICIOUS BEAST**. I won't have it! Go on, out you go!"

Once again, he is chased out to the back step.

He's still recovering when, a few seconds after, Mrs Grout opens the door and puts his breakfast down with a clang, muttering all the while.

Danny eats the food and then does what a dog's got to do. As he is weeing up against a tree, he wonders how Dudley will cope with doing what a boy's got to do... This doesn't really bear thinking about!

Searching around the garden, he looks for gaps in the fence that might let him escape, but no. Dad plugged up all the holes ages ago when Dudley was a puppy and kept escaping into a neighbour's garden, digging up their flowerbeds and scoffing their prize-winning vegetables.

Coming over to the back door, Danny can see Mrs Grout inside. She's talking to someone and patting the back of her hair. She turns around and her expression looks weird. It takes a minute for Danny to realise this is her happy face.

When the other person moves in front of the glass door, Danny's tail starts to wag. It's Phil the window cleaner. He has only just started doing their windows and is always friendly to Danny, sometimes giving him a sweet when Mum isn't looking.

Mrs Grout goes to her handbag on the table and takes out a big envelope of money with *CASH FOR DECORATORS* written on the front. She gives Phil three ten-pound notes then puts the envelope back in her bag.

The door opens and Phil comes out, holding his ladder and a bucket of water.

"Thanks for that, Mrs G," he says over his shoulder. "It'll be a nice surprise when they get back. These windows will be gleaming by the time I've finished." He sees Danny. "'Ello, old boy."

Phil squats down and scratches under Danny's chin. (*Darn*, that feels good.)

"You've got to help me!" says Danny, but all that comes out is frantic woofing. "Mrs Grout's going to get rid of me today! You've got to do something!"

"Now, now, then, what's all this barking about?" says Phil mildly, giving Danny a rub under the ears.

"**NO!** You're not *listening*..."

Mrs Grout opens the back door.

"I wish that animal would stop its noise. It's giving me a headache. And the smell! How can you stand it?"

Phil shrugs and gets to his feet.

"It's just a nice doggy sort of smell," he says. "Well, these windows aren't going to clean themselves are they, Mrs G?"

"I'll let you get on," says Mrs Grout cheerfully. Then she looks down at Danny and her smile switches off like a light. "Anyway," she says quietly, "not long now until I get you sorted too."

Heart thumping, Danny looks into her eyes and gives her the most powerful death stare he can manage. He hears a deep, rumbling growl come out of his mouth. But this time, it is exactly what he means to do.

7

No morning dinner.

No walkies.

No sniff.

No Danny.

Dudley is fed up, even if it *is* comfy here
on the bed. (He lay on it ALL NIGHT long
and no one shouted at him once!) He gives an
experimental whine to make his feelings known.

"Look, it won't be long until breakfast,"
says the Dad. "You've already eaten all the

complimentary biscuits so you'll just have to be patient."

Dudley is distracted from his thoughts by the door opening and some people coming in. There are loud voices about "terrible roadworks on the by-pass" and "thought we were never going to get here!"

He gives a little bark to hurry everyone along. They all ignore him so he skulks off by the window, trying to lie nose-to-tail in a comforting circle. Dudley whines sadly.

A Danny-sized girl with long hair and brown eyes comes over and peers at him, her expression frowny. She has a scrunched-up piece of paper in her hand and is bouncing it and catching it again. Dudley can't stop watching this.

Up.

Catch.

Up.

Catch.

47

Then she kicks the piece of paper neatly into a wastepaper bin, before bending down to look into Dudley's face.

"What are you doing?" she says. "Are you pretending to be a dog?"

Dudley tries to bark her away but all that comes out is, "**DUDLEY!**"

The girl spends ages staring at him then.

She turns her head one way and then the other way as if she is thinking through something very difficult. A bit like when Dudley is waiting for dinner, but Danny starts a game of tug with his toy rope and he doesn't know which thing to want the most.

"Wait a minute," she says finally, looking at him so close up that Dudley can see tiny boys that look just like Danny reflected in her eyes. (Eh?) "Are you...? Hang on, that can't be..."

"**DUDLEY!**" he barks again, and she almost falls over.

"Blimey," she said quietly, "I don't think you're pretending, are you?"

The girl sits on the floor to talk to Dudley and tells him her name is Priya. She says some other things that Dudley doesn't listen to because he's too busy sniffing her. Even with a broken sniff, she smells like a friend.

FINALLY all of them – the Priya, the Mum and the Dad and the others – leave the room and go into a big place that is absolutely teeming with delicious foody smells.

The Priya sticks close to him *and* calls him by his proper name.

"Now then, Dudley," she whispers. "I'm going to look after you and it will be— **NO! DON'T DO THAT!**"

All he'd done was try to stick his nose in a lovely big dish of eggy-stuff on a long table. And wait … is that…? Is that … *SAUSAGES*?! But, oh no, not for Dudley.

"This is called a breakfast buffet," says the Priya quietly, pulling him away. "And I'm going to get you a big plate of food while you *sit* nicely on this chair, OK? *Sit!*"

Dudley knows how to do that. He looks down at the funny pink things he has instead of paws, to pass the time. Come to think of it, these look a bit like sausages. Maybe they taste like them too? Giving them a little lick he thinks, *not bad, but nowhere near as good as real ones.*

The Dad sits down with a lovely big plate of morning-dinner and says, "Stop eating your own fingers. You can't be that hungry."

Which is just a silly thing to say. Of course Dudley can.

He gives a sad whine.

Where's his morning-dinner?

Where's his Danny?

And **HIS SNIFF IS STILL GONE!**

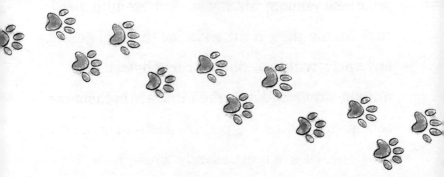

8

Danny is lying by the back door when Mrs Grout clips the dog lead onto his collar.

"Come on then," says Mrs Grout, hurriedly standing back again. "I promised I'd walk you so I'd better do it."

She's behaving strangely. Danny can hear her heart thudding beneath her pink jumper and she's acting twitchy. It's a puzzle but he's too distracted by what his own body is doing to think about Mrs Grout.

For some reason just hearing the word "walk" makes his tail wag *all on its own*, which is most peculiar. His boy-body doesn't really do things without his say-so. But for all his tail says *yes*, Danny's brain says *no*. He's not going anywhere with *her*. She'll probably walk him miles away from home then leave him there or something, telling his parents he has run off.

Nope. He's staying exactly where he is. He looks up at her defiantly.

"Move, you **SILLY** beast!" says Mrs Grout.

She gives the lead a slight tug.

Not happening.

"Come *on*! I haven't got all day!"

Danny lays his head on his paws and pretends to go to sleep to make his point. But then Mrs Grout gives a lead a great big pull.

Hang on...

Danny feels himself move a little bit, the floor tiles slippery below him. He can't stop it!

"A-ha!" says Mrs Grout, pulling so hard now that Danny's whole doggy body begins to slide slowly across the floor like a huge, hairy mop.

He tries to resist. It's a one-woman, one-dog tug-of-war. But even though he is a big dog, Mrs Grout is a bigger woman. She is winning. Before long Danny has slid all the way to the front door.

"Ha!" says Mrs Grout triumphantly. "Enough of this nonsense. It's time for **WALKIES!**"

Not on your life, Danny thinks. But his treacherous tail starts wagging all by itself *again*!

Admitting defeat, he leaves the house and mooches along the road, trying not to be too distracted by all the amazing smells bombarding him from every direction. Someone is cooking a delicious-smelling curry in one house, bacon and eggs in another, pancakes and hazelnut spread further along... A man walks by eating gum and Danny is blasted with minty freshness.

How does Dudley *cope* with all these pongs? Smelling is a full-time job for a dog.

Danny's still musing on this when he spies a tall, thin whippet walking towards him from the other direction. Danny's senses go into overdrive. He can see the dog, smell the dog – a mixture of fish, feet and mud (strangely delicious) – and hear its heart beating all at once. The whippet gives him a very snooty look as it walks by, almost like it knows he's not a real dog. Before he can stop himself, Danny is turning towards the other dog's rear end.

Oh please. No, I'm not really going to—

But oh yes. He really is…

"**DIRTY BEAST!**" Mrs Grout cries.
Danny's nose is a centimetre from sniffing the
other dog's bottom when she yanks him away.

"Ugh! Honestly, dogs are so *disgusting*! I
might not be able to do anything about your
dirty habits but there are other things I can fix!"

That's when Danny makes a decision (even
though he is reeling a bit from the whole almost-
sniffing-another-dog's-bum thing).

If he can get off this lead, he *will* make a run
for it.

9

Dudley is trying to make his ears flat to show how he feels about this disappointing day.

The Mum had got cross with him. "For goodness sake, why am I having to dress you? You're not that poorly, surely?"

The Dad had got cross with him. "Poorly? Never bloomin' seen a boy eat breakfast so quickly. Didn't think it was possible to get scrambled egg on your forehead."

The Priya hadn't got cross, but kept standing

very close and looking at him like he was the very strangest dog she had ever seen.

He has had no walkies *at all*, not even "just around the streets because there's no time for the park today". He keeps pulling at the uncomfortable new collar that the Mum made him wear. He wishes he had his old collar on, the one with the hanging thing that goes *clink! clink!* against his water bowl when he has a drink.

He misses his water bowl.

Now they are in a big room that smells of **COLD** and **OLD**. The Priya had sat very close to Dudley in the car, saying things in a quiet, soft voice like, "Now then, Dudley, this is the wedding part of the day. You have to sit and not do any barking or licking or anything at all, OK?"

Lot of people are sitting in rows. Dudley is squashed between the Priya and the Mum. Music starts to play and a lady with a big white sprouty thing on her head is walking past holding onto a man's arm. They are both smiling but, even so, they look like they need a poo.

A small person like a puppy-human is walking next to them holding lots of tasty garden things.

"She's the flower girl," Priya whispers.

The flowers look yummy. Dudley leans over to take a tiny nibble. The puppy-girl yaps and shoves him hard.

It is all very strange. No one seems to want to play with him today.

By the time it all finishes and they go back to the Big House, Dudley is **FED UP**. Now everyone is standing

around in a big room and people are HA-HA-HA-ing VERY LOUDLY. When is next dinner? Dudley barks at the Priya to ask but her eyes go wide and she makes shushy noises and flaps her hands.

That's when Dudley sees something watching him from just inside the doorway to the big room.

It's not a human but it's not a dog either. The not-dog is one of those fluffy, spitting **ENEMY** creatures. They are not to be trusted because:

1) They don't like him. (Dudley know this because they always hiss at him.)

2) They smell funny.

3) (Hmm … mainly the first thing, now he thinks about it.)

"Uh oh," says the Priya. "A cat. Can you just ignore—?"

But Dudley isn't listening. He must defend everyone from the Enemy! It might be a big boring room filled with HA-HA-HA people but it's his, *Dudley's,* big boring room with all the HA-HA-HA people!

Dudley chases after the Enemy at top speed, smashing into something hard that falls in pieces that go *clang! clang! clang!* all over the ground.

Dudley clambers over them all and keeps on running, tongue out. He is a determined Dudley.

"That child has just destroyed a fifteenth-century suit of armour!" shouts someone.

"Stop him!" shouts another.

"**WATCH OUT!** We're bringing the wedding cake through!" shouts someone else.

CRASH!

Dudley has lost the Enemy. And lots of people are all shouting at once, but he's landed in a huge pile of something that tastes like the best thing ever! Dudley gets stuck in, gobbling down as much of it as he can before he's being hauled away by his collar so fast his feet skid all over the floor.

Mrs Grout kept Danny firmly on the lead for the entire walk.

Since they got back, he has been thinking about how he can get away. Now he might have a chance: Mrs Grout is signing for a package.

Just beyond Mrs Grout is the postman and just beyond *him* lies glorious **FREEDOM**.

It's now or never!

As he shoots towards the open door, Mrs Grout attempts to tackle him but, even though

Danny is rubbish at football, he is determined.
Put it this way: even if the best defenders in
the world were in front of him right now, they
couldn't defeat him. He runs past Mrs Grout,
past the postman...

And he's **FREE**!

All the way to the bottom of the street,
Danny can hear Mrs Grout shouting and his tail
wags with joy. He skids on his paws when he
gets to the corner and turns to sprint down the
street.

Ears flying in the wind, heart pounding and
tongue out, Danny gets to the park in no time.
He's never run so fast in his life and he takes a

minute to catch his breath, looking around at a familiar place that now seems so different.

He can still remember getting to the top of that climbing frame for the first time and feeling he had conquered Mount Everest. And those swings, where he jumped off at the top of a big push and scraped all the skin off one of his knees. He wouldn't be allowed in that bit as a dog, that's for sure. But there is another part of the park where dogs can go. A few people are sitting on the grass. He doesn't pay them much attention as he sniffs for the right place (funny how he just KNOWS) and has a celebratory wee against a park bench.

He'll hide in here as long as he has to.

Mum and Dad (and Dudley, which is too weird to think about right now) will be back tomorrow, so all Danny has to do is stay out for one night.

He tries to picture normal weekends. What if he never gets to have one again as a boy? Swimming first thing. Massive fry up for lunch. Playing a game on his Switch in the afternoon and movie night with pizza at the end. If he's still a dog, how will that work?

The thought of normal makes him sad for a second but then he hears *thwack-thump*, followed by happy shouting.

A group of kids a bit older than him have arrived in the park with a football.

Danny can feel his fur rising in excitement along his back.

But hang on, he doesn't even *like* football. Whenever his mates at school or his cousin Priya go on about football, then Danny switches off. Apparently his doggy brain hasn't got that memo. Now he is running towards that ball as if his life depends on it. Diving into the middle of the game, he sinks his teeth into the football, feeling a strangely satisfying *puff* of air.

Oops. Might have punctured it.

Never mind! This is the **BEST FOOTBALL GAME EVER!**

There is a lot of shouting. One big teenage boy tries to grab his collar. But Danny can't seem to stop running around in circles. It's such **FUN**.

As someone grabs hold of his back legs, another wrestles the ball from his mouth.

"Look what this dog did to the ball!"

He feels his ears flattening. He really *hadn't* meant to break it. Maybe this is why Dudley sometimes does naughty things? It just feels too good to resist? It's so strange. He thinks like Danny, but Dudley's body is in the driving seat and making him act in very un-Dannyish ways.

He stares down so all he can see is a ring of different sorts of trainers around him.

"This dog's owner owes me a new football!" says someone. "Where are they anyway?"

Danny decides it is time to get away, so he pushes through a gap in the legs and gets ready to slink off and hide somewhere.

That's when there is an excited yelp from nearby and he is suddenly enveloped in a pair of small, chubby arms.

"**Doddy! Duddy!**"

Oh no. It's Holly from down the road, here with her mum. Holly always gets very over-excited when she sees Dudley – Dudley always tries to hide behind Danny's legs. But where can *Danny* hide?

"Holly! Holly, come back! We don't know that doggy!" says her mum.

"Duddy!" Holly screeches again, battering him on the back with a pudgy fist. Her mother charges over.

"Come away from that dog at once, Holly!"

"**Doddy! DUDDY!**" says the little girl, more desperately now.

"Get off!" cries Danny, but all that comes out is excited barking.

"Oh, I recognize you! It's Danny Pond's dog, isn't it?" says Holly's mum, but Danny is distracted by the extraordinarily painful thing happening just above his ear, right where Holly has one of her chubby hands.

"Oh, Holly," says her mother, shaking her head. "Look, you've gone and got your lolly stuck in the dog's fur." When she tries to take it out, it feels as though someone is pulling Danny's skin off bit by painful bit and he howls in response.

"Oh dear, I think we'd better see if Danny's mummy can cut it out. Come on, let's get you home, boy."

Danny looks around wildly for an escape route but Holly's mum is already slipping her long blue scarf through his collar as a makeshift lead.

Walking back to the house with the scarf tied

to the side of Holly's buggy, Danny attempts a few pulls. Holly cackles with glee and shouts, **"AGAIN, DUDDY!"** as her buggy wobbles.

Danny can't believe how horrible a sight his own front door can be. But it's even worse when Mrs Grout opens it and glares down at him.

"Oh," says Holly's mum, her friendly smile faltering. "Is Annie home? Or Kev? Only we found their dog in the park."

"They're away," says Mrs Grout, baring her teeth in one of her terrifying grins. "This ... scamp ... ran off. The naughty boy."

Danny cowers as she bends towards him menacingly.

"He's a naughty boy! Yes he is! Who's a naughty boy, then? You are!"

You're fooling no-one, thinks Danny. Mrs Grout starts scratching his ears, her mouth only a very small squiggle of disgust. Then she gives a little shriek.

"**Eurghh!** What's that in its fur?"

"I'm afraid my daughter's lolly got stuck," says Holly's mum apologetically. "If you could—"

"Not to worry," says Mrs Grout. She hands back the scarf and pulls Danny inside by the collar. "Thank you for bringing the dog back."

The door closes. She glares down at him, looking as big as a skyscraper. Danny slinks low on the mat.

"Now then," Mrs Grout says in a quiet, creepy voice. "I don't think we'll need to worry about sticky fur, will we? Not where you're going."

Danny gulps. He was right. This is it.

Mrs Grout really *is* going to get rid of him. It wasn't an idle threat. She means business.

He wishes so badly that it was a normal Saturday, and he was a boy and Dudley was safe.

But *you* know what happened the last time he made a wish: he ended up in this mess.

11

Cross, whispery voices everywhere.

No one likes Dudley.

"So not only do I have to cough up for a priceless suit of armour ..." (the Dad) "...we have to pay for an entire wedding cake too!"

"That's not even the worst bit!" (The Mum.) "It's the *humiliation*! What *is* wrong with you, Danny? We can never show our flipping faces again!"

They are standing in the corridor just outside

the big room full of people. Dudley hangs his
head in shame, longing to slink away to his very
own lovely bed, with all its happy, comforting
smells, where he could curl up and sleep away
all this bother.

"We really would have been better off
bringing Dudley with us!" says the Dad.

DUDLEY!

They do like
him after all!
Dudley leaps up
and gives the
Dad a big lick
on his chin. The
Dad's face has
gone funny so he
obviously likes it.

"What the—
what did he—?"
he splutters.

The Priya suddenly appears from round the corner.

"Sorry for listening in!" she says. "But I have a theory."

"A theory about what?" says the Mum. The Dad is still looking funny and doesn't speak.

"I think somehow," says the Priya, "and you have to just stay with me here, I think that *somehow* Dudley is in control of Danny's brain and *not* Danny!"

"That's the daftest thing I have ever heard," says the Dad after a moment of silence.

"Maybe…" says the Priya. "But look at all the evidence." She begins to count on her fingers. "One, there's the way he tried to curl up on the floor when I arrived. Two, he tried to eat breakfast without using his cutlery *or* his hands, just his mouth. Three, he chased a cat and –" she counts off the last finger – "four, he just tried to lick your face!"

"Hmm... I wasn't going to mention this,"
says the Dad. "But this morning, I caught him
cocking his leg *against the bath*! I had to show
him how to use the toilet like he was three years
old again!"

The room is silent. The big humans and the
Priya are all looking at Dudley. Self-conscious
now, he wants to scratch
his ears but
his back leg
won't ... quite
... reach. He
collapses in a
heap.

"**SEE!**"
cries the
Priya.

12

Worst. Day. Ever.

Mrs Grout is watching him like a hawk. The front door stays tightly shut. Every now and then she looks at the big clock in the hall and says things like "Not long to go now!" and "Roll on three o'clock..."

Danny looks at the clock as well: two o'clock.

Just one hour until ... what? Will she take him somewhere and simply let him go? Push him in the river?

Danny is a good swimmer but Dudley is scared of water.

Dad once said, "So we have a dog that doesn't bring back sticks, won't do any tricks and can't swim. Does it do anything a dog is meant to do? Apart from dig up all my flowerbeds?"

This is quite a puzzle now Danny thinks about it. Would his real *Danny*-mind help him swim? Or will his *Dudley*-body let him down? Even though Danny is quite good at breast stroke and even butterfly, would he have to doggy paddle? Or would he just sink?

It's so complicated it is giving him a headache. Plus he still has a lolly stuck in his fur. He'd quite like to eat it, actually, but can't reach.

Danny is sleepy too. Finally he understands why Dudley spends hours napping every day. It's exhausting being a dog. He could lay his head down for a moment and...

NO!

MUST STAY AWAKE!

He gets up and does some circuits of the downstairs rooms to keep himself busy. Mrs Grout is hoovering something to death upstairs and can't tell him off.

Danny is circling round the dining room at the back of the house when he sees a movement at the window.

Phil the window cleaner is peering in. It's so nice to see his friendly face that Danny feels a waggy tail coming on.

Shading his eyes with a hand, Phil seems to be looking for something. Then he seems to spot whatever it is because he gives a small nod. Confused, Danny looks around the room. Everything looks the same as normal. Mrs Grout has a whole load of cleaning products on the table next to her handbag but what's unusual about that? (Nothing.) When Phil sees Dudley he gives him a big smile and a wave.

Is Phil making sure he is OK? Perhaps he suspects Mrs Grout's evil nature? Maybe Phil is going to keep an eye out and make sure nothing happens?

It's a surprise but a very nice one. Good old Phil. Who knew he was a secret dog-saving hero?

Flumping down in a splash of warm sunlight on the floor, Danny decides maybe he can relax. Just for five minutes...

AT LAST! WALKIES!

"Now then, Dudders," says the Priya as they head onto some grass at the back of the big building. "I don't think they believe me about this whole boy-dog-swap business. But we all agree that you need a bit of a run around. Maybe you'll calm down a bit!" She pauses. "So," she says. "Here are some ground rules: no peeing on things; no digging things up; no scoffing anything you find on the ground. Got it?"

Huh, thinks Dudley. Not much of a walk. Those are all the best bits! But he's very keen to avoid any more cross voices, so he trots off and soon busies himself sniffing around a bin. Funny, but it doesn't smell quite as good as normal. In fact ... it smells ... bad?

"Nothing to see here!" the Priya is saying to a couple of humans with enormous hats who

are staring at him strangely. "My cousin is just looking for something he lost, that's all!"

She's making a quiet HA-HA noise as she comes over and pulls him away by his funny sausage paws.

"Maybe you can just be a good boy for five minutes?" she says.

Dudley wants to be a good boy. He really does.

The Priya has found a tennis ball now and is throwing it up, kicking it with her foot, then catching it. Dudley is QUITE interested in this but his brain is still hurty with the Question of the Bin. Why does it not smell nice today? Is it because of the broken sniff? Maybe he should give it another go? There is usually something tasty inside bins, isn't there?

He creeps back over and leans in to get a much better sniff. No. Still bad. Maybe he can just reach down a little further and...

OOPS!

The Priya is peering down at him. "Are you serious right now? Am I actually going to have to get you out of *a bin*?!"

Danny wakes up with a gasp, heart thumping. He'd been dreaming he was tied to a goalpost while Mrs Grout kicked footballs at him.

He shoots into the kitchen to look at the clock.

And gasps. (Or tries to.)

It's two minutes to three! Even with his boy-thoughts inside Dudley's dog-body he hasn't been able to outwit Mrs Grout and escape. Poor Dudley. *And poor me!*

Danny runs to the back door and scratches at it, whining. She'll have to let him out if he needs a wee, won't she? And then he will get away somehow.

"Come on, then," Mrs Grout says. "You'd better do your filthy business quickly. And this time, there will be no funny business."

She clips on the lead before Danny can blink. As she drags him down the back steps, he notices a ladder propped up at the side of the house. Phil must have left it behind by accident. But his view is blocked because Mrs Grout is towering over him, her hands on her hips.

"Go on then!" she hisses.

He wants to say, "Well, I can't go with you hovering over me, can I?" but knows it will only come out as *woof-woof-woof*.

"You don't need to go at all do you? **SILLY DOG!** Now get back inside. It's almost time."

As she drags him back into the house,

Danny hears the most horrible, spine-tingling sound.

The doorbell.

Fear gives him super strength and before Mrs Grout can stop him, Danny pulls the lead from her hands and shoots off up the stairs and into his bedroom where he can see out of the window.

There is a white van parked outside the house. He can't quite make out the writing on the side and tries jumping up and down to catch glimpses of it. When the words come into view, he feels his tummy drop as though he were in a lift.

PEST CONTROL?

Danny knows that pest control people come to your house and lay down poison for rats or mice. They get rid of cockroaches and ants and all sorts of unwanted creatures.

Unwanted creatures like ... a big, grey hairy mutt that's part Labrador, part poodle, part rug and (now) part boy?

Dudley is tired.

There hasn't been *nearly* enough dinner today. When it finally arrived, Dudley tried to put his face in the bowl to lap up the nice-smelling wet stuff. But the Mum and the Dad had gone, "Use your **SPOON** for soup!" at exactly the same time. Luckily the Priya showed him what to do with his funny paws but if you asked Dudley, that was a silly way to eat things. Not that anyone *is* asking Dudley.

He slumps down in his chair and makes himself as small as he can.

There had been lots of talking after the disappointingly small dinner and now it's all YAK-YAK-YAK and HA-HA-HA. Some people are doing funny movements on a floor with lights on it too.

The Priya sees him looking and says, "That's called 'dancing'. It's not a very good example."

Someone comes up to speak to her then. They say, "They should win that, because Arsenal are good at home." And a moment later the Priya says, "He's not really a first team player but he's pretty good coming off the bench."

And for one lovely moment no one has their eyes on Dudley.

Sliding down the chair v-e-r-y- s-l-o-w-l-y Dudley slips under the table. There's a big white cloth hiding him, but he can see all the leggies and human paws of all the people from down here, stretching into the distance.

But wait, what's that? The spitting-hissing monster is across the room, smirking and licking its back leg like it owns the place.

NO. Dudley's not having it. Must see it off. It's his doggy duty.

He shoots out from under the table, knocking over some chairs on the way.

People are shouting now. At him?

NO!

Something else is happening that isn't important enough to distract him – a funny smell and a warm feeling on his face – but Dudley won't let that put him off.

"*The candles!*" says someone.

"*Her dress is on fire!*" says another.

"*Somebody help her!*"

Dudley is focused on the Enemy. He hurls himself forwards just as the not-dog jumps on a table to get away from him...

Two can play at that game! Dudley jumps too. He is a flying dog!

NEEEEEAAAWWWW!

But he is coming into land now, heading straight for a huge white pot of sprouty garden stuff. It's balanced on a table next to people flapping their arms and shouting. "Fire! Fire!"

16

It is like a nightmare – but you can wake up from nightmares. There is no escape from this.

Mrs Grout opens the door and greets a blonde woman dressed in white overalls with a picture of a dog on the pocket.

Maybe they exterminate dogs all the time! The whole rat/cockroach thing is obviously just a cover. She is smiling in a friendly way as though she isn't really an evil dog killer.

She bends down and says, "So is this the

fella we're having this afternoon, then? I can see you're in need of the treatment." Danny growls and her eyebrows shoot up. "Oh, like that is it? Well, don't worry, it will be over in no time."

The fact that it will be quick doesn't make Danny feel better.

Before he knows it, he is being bundled into a cage in the back of the van. Danny presses his nose against the window and looks at his house for the last time, whimpering. The van speeds up and the house gets smaller and smaller.

Goodbye, house.

Goodbye, Mum and Dad.

Goodbye, Dudley, bestest dog and bestest friend in the world.

After just a few minutes the van comes to a shuddering stop.

The doors open with a clang and the blonde woman is smiling at him again. She doesn't *look* evil but looks can't be trusted.

"Now, boy," she says, "let's get you sorted
out, shall we?"

He tries to charge past her, but she is much
stronger than she looks (see!) and easily gets him
onto the lead and down onto the street.

"HELP, HELP!" cries Danny. "There
is an evil plan to get me exterminated!" But of
course, all that comes out is *BARK, BARK, BARK*.

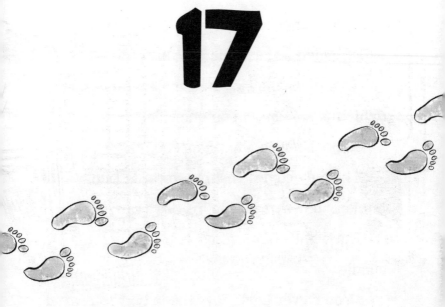

So much LOUD.

Dudley tries to make himself small.

There has been all sorts of shrieking and shouting, and a lady is patting at her big white dress that is all wet. The air smells of **HOT** and also of **WET**.

He tries to work out what happened …

… he was chasing the hissing spitting monster …

… and he jumped onto the table …

… and knocked over that big white pot, which made water come gushing out …

… all over the lady in the big white dress (which is now brown on one side).

Nope. No idea what happened there.

The lady comes rushing towards Dudley. He hunkers down as low as his body can go.

But what's happening? Is he getting … a cuddle?

"You clever boy!" says the lady. "You saved me! Such quick thinking! To pour the water from the flower display onto my dress like that and stop it going up like a torch!"

"Oh, darling, you could have been seriously injured! I'm so sorry!" says a man, coming over and putting his hand on her shoulder. "You're a very good boy, Danny. You've saved my *wife* –" everyone starts clapping at this bit and going HAHAHAHA again – "from being badly hurt!"

He's the Good Boy! **FINALLY!**

He licks the lady's hand, and no one even gets cross.

This has turned into the **BEST DAY EVER!**

18

The woman has brought Danny inside a building where lots of people are sitting around with dogs.

There are big brown dogs with nice faces and small white dogs that look like their faces got squashed. There are skinny grey dogs with

long noses and ears like ladies' hair and chunky striped dogs with wonky eyes. Every single one of them is looking at Danny. He can sense the same thing as with that whippet on his walk – no, he can *smell* it – they don't really trust him. They somehow know he's not the same as them. The other dogs even move away from him a tiny bit. Maybe he smells just a little bit of Boy, despite it all?

"Oh, who do we have here, then?"

Danny looks up to see a lady with black hair dressed in a plastic apron and gloves and wearing a huge smile.

"This is Dudley," says the blonde woman, passing over the lead. "Full treatment for him, Glenda."

"Right you are, Sally," says Glenda, taking him through some doors.

Danny closes his eyes. This is it. The end. *At least this isn't happening to you, Dudley*, he thinks as he is pushed forwards to his fate.

Goodbye, world.

"No need to whine!" says Glenda. "I'll make sure the water is just right."

He opens one eye and feels a pleasant sensation down his back. Warm water all over his body. Around the room, dogs are covered in soapy foam and something nice-smelling is in the steamy air. It is only then he sees the sign on the wall and...

Things make sense for the first time today.

The name on the van wasn't 'Pest Control'. It was *Pet Central*. On the sign, it says *For all your animal's needs!*

So that was Mrs Grout's plan. She just wanted Dudley to have a bath all along!

"There now, boy, that's not so bad, is it?" says Glenda and Danny gives a happy bark for the first time.

Then he gets a brilliant idea.

He twists one way and then the other unleashing the biggest, wettest, shakiest, messiest and most satisfying dog shake ever. He's **ALWAYS** wanted to do that!

19

Dudley can't believe he's allowed on the bed for *another* night. Maybe it is because everyone thinks he is the Good Boy now? (He has really suspected this for years, deep down.)

He has eaten so much cake that he has almost stopped feeling hungry.

If it wasn't for the broken sniff and missing Danny so much, he would be a very happy dog.

The Mum kept saying things like, "My brave boy! You're a hero!" and the Dad said, "Well done, son. Obviously a chip off the old block."

After such a long day, Dudley needs a long sleep and he snuggles on the bed, trying to go nose-to-tail before remembering he can't. His eyes are too sleepy to stay open but then he hears talking and his ears prick.

"Darling," says the Mum. "I know this makes no sense, but do you think Priya could possibly be right?"

What's that? Dudley strains his hearing flappers.

"I don't know," says the Dad. "I'm starting to wonder the same thing. If it wasn't the daftest theory I'd ever heard, I would think that was *Dudley* lying over there right now, rather than our boy."

There is a low *ha-ha* sound.

"I can't believe I'm saying this,' says the Mum. "But I know exactly what you mean."

Silly humans, thinks Dudley. Of course it's Dudley. Who else could it be?

20

Back in London, a boy's mind trapped inside a dog's brain is trying to sleep.

He'd ended up having a brilliant time at Pet Central, tomorrow everyone was coming home and things would be OK again.

Wouldn't they?

But now he doesn't have to worry about Mrs Grout all his fears about being a dog have crowded in. What if he is trapped inside Dudley's body **FOR EVER?**

How did he even get this way? He tries to remember... He'd been wishing really hard on the Pup Star... Maybe that was all he had to do to be Danny again? Or maybe if some of the stardust was inside him, all he had to do was wish?

He gets out of bed and pads upstairs to his real Danny-bedroom. Looking out of the window with his paws on the windowsill, he searches for the star. But it's too cloudy to see anything much tonight.

Defeated, he jumps onto his proper Boy Bed, and turns a circle before settling down. He's bound to sleep better here and, if Mrs Grout tells him off in the morning, who cares? He has a feeling she might even let it go now he's all clean because Danny has worked something out about Mrs Grout. That funny vinegary smell from before? (That stung his nostrils and made him nervous. Who knew emotions had a smell?!) Something tells him it was *fear*. Maybe Mrs Grout was scared of Dudley? It seems to have gone now she's more used to him. Hard to understand but, Danny has to admit, when Dudley comes to say "hello" it's like being hit by a hairy rocket. Maybe that was the cause of all the squinching and flapping and frowning? That ... and the fact that maybe (if he's being honest) Dudley is a bit smelly.

Anyway, he's too tired to think about it any more. The bed smells of home, safety and comfort. His eyes are beginning to droop when all his senses crackle to life.

There's a sweaty smell but it's not in the room. It's outside. Danny's ears twitch at what sounds like a twig cracking ever so gently in the garden.

Someone's out there!

Then everything happens very fast. There's a scratching, metallic sound and a pale face stares in through the window. Now a hand is reaching through the open top part of the window and reaching down to undo the latch.

The window swings wide open. Danny watches in amazement as the arms then head and shoulders of a man emerge into the room. The sweat smell is really strong now. He looks up and Danny sees it is Phil the window cleaner! He's breaking in! Noticing Danny on the bed, he flinches then starts whispering gently to him.

"OK, boy, who's a good boy then? It's just your old friend Phil, nothing to worry about. Look, I've got you some treats." Phil creeps over to the bed and scatters a handful of what looks like doggie chocs onto the duvet. "Now then, boy, you just eat those."

But when Danny sniffs them, they don't smell right at all.

Instinct tells him to pretend to eat the chocs.

He moves his mouth over them as though gobbling them up.

"That's it ... you'll soon be fast asleep, you horrible mutt," whispers Phil and leaves the room, slowly creeping down the stairs.

Danny goes after him too shocked to do anything else.

Phil is reaching for something on the table.

Danny's jaw drops open in shock because Phil is now rooting around inside Mrs Grout's handbag.

The person who gives him sweets and pretends to like dogs is a **THIEF!**

Danny gives a low growl deep in this throat and Phil looks up, an ugly expression on his face.

"Shut it, mutt," he says and looks back inside the bag. He holds up the envelope of money in Mrs Grout's bag and smiles a nasty smile. "There you are, my beauty," he whispers before shoving it in his pocket and making his way back to the stairs.

"MRS GROUT! MRS GROUT! **WE'RE BEING BURGLED!**" shouts Danny finally finding his voice. (Well, his bark.) Phil whirls round and tries to kick Danny but Danny dodges him and bounces around his feet, shouting at the top of his lungs.

"What is all that barking for, you silly dog?" Mrs Grout calls from the spare room. "Just be quiet and go to sleep!"

Danny chases Phil back into his own room. Phil is now squeezing himself back through the window.

There is only one thing for it.

Danny closes his eyes, takes a deep breath ... and sinks his teeth into Phil's bottom as it starts to disappear through the window.

"**YOWWWWWWWWW!**" screams Phil, hopping around and trying to shake him off, but Danny holds on even though Phil's bottom is the very worst thing he's ever tasted.

"Is someone there?" shouts Mrs Grout in a shaky voice, then she emerges at the bedroom door and lets out an ear-splitting scream.

Danny is still holding on for grim life a minute later when he hears, "Hello, is that the police? I want to report a burglar!"

DUDLEY'S HOUSE!

He's so excited he doesn't know what to do
first. Sniff his lovely bed? Check his bowl in case
some dinner has miraculously appeared? Look
for his best friend Danny?

In the end he does all those things in a
series of frantic circles but it's a bit distracting
because there's *another dog* sitting in the
hallway of *his* house and the dog is staring right
at him.

A really *silly* looking dog too, Dudley thinks
sniffily. So glad HE doesn't look half that
ridiculous. He trots over with his head held high
then bends down to give it a good sniff.

Something familiar there...

Does he know this dog?

It's the strangest feeling ever, Danny thinks, looking up at his own self. And let's face it, after the last couple of days, that's saying something.

A flash of panic. What if Dudley isn't in there after all?

But the boy has an unmistakably goofy look about him, which Danny is quite sure *he* doesn't have in normal life. He is further reassured when the boy gets down and begins sniffing him all over.

A boy sniffing a dog would have looked very strange indeed but, luckily, Mum and Dad are distracted by hearing all about the robbery. Mrs Grout had a phone call from the police to say that Phil is safely in custody.

Looking at his own body in front of him, Danny is suddenly overcome with longing for his own arms and legs and trainers with lighting-up bits, instead of fur and claws and a waggy tail. (Even though he has to admit that shaking wet fur over everyone was fun.)

When Danny goes back to the dog basket, the boy follows him and tries to get in the basket with him. Surely Dudley wants his body back too?

Danny wishes as hard as he can, with every wishing molecule in his body.

"*On the Pup Star, let me be Danny again, let me be Danny again. PLEASE let me be Danny again.*" Then he gives the boy the biggest, wettest lick he can muster.

There is a yappy whooshing sound, the same as before, and the first thing Danny is aware of again is a **HORRIBLE FISHY SMELL** on his face.

The hairy, loveable face of his best friend gazes up at him with a very relieved expression in his eyes.

Danny looks down and gives himself a quick once over.

Boy arms? **Check**.

Boy legs? **Check**.

Blue trainers with lighting-up bits? **Check**.

"We've had quite an eventful weekend too," Mum is saying, "although I think Danny has been having some funny turns."

"It's OK, Mum," says Danny quietly. "I'm back. It's me!"

His mum blinks hard a few times and then rushes over to hug him.

"And doesn't Dudders look lovely!" she manages to say, even though her voice has gone all funny. "Did you give him a bath, Mrs Grout?"

Mrs Grout looks down at the dog, who is happily sniffing his bottom and, this time, the usual squiggle of disgust is almost gone.

"Yes, I hope you don't mind," she says. "We've become quite good friends, me and Dudley." She looks down for a moment. "I know it's silly but I think I was a bit scared of him before. He's so big and, um, enthusiastic. But," she smiles. (And maybe she doesn't look so weird this time.) "You're a good boy really, aren't you? If I hadn't had that big envelope of money to pay the painters in my bag, it would never have happened. But Dudley saved the day!"

Everyone stands around grinning for a few moments and feeling pleased with themselves.

Until a horrible smell starts to tickle their noses.

They start laughing, then…

"OH, DUDLEY!"

Dudley gives a happy bark at the sound of his name. Everyone must like him a lot because they are saying his name, all at once!

He barks again, this time to tell them something really important.

They can stop worrying.

His sniff has come back!